Razor Wire Pubic Hair

an anti-novel of the future

by

Carlton Mellick III

ERASERHEAD PRESS

RAZOR WIRE PUBIC HAIR

Copyright © 2003 by Carlton Mellick III

Cover art copyright © 2003 by Steven Stahlberg

ISBN: 0-9729598-1-5

Eraserhead Press
16455 E. Fairlynn Dr,
Fountain Hills, AZ 85268

email: publisher@eraserheadpress.com

website: www.eraserheadpress.com

Author's Note

I wrote this book while living in dream worlds at age 23. It is all just sex. It is not porn, not erotica, but all sex. It explores some hidden/unpopular sides of sex: the crude, painful, passionate, awkward, uplifting, obsessive, nightmarish, childish, boring, spiteful, philosophical, artistic, and funny sides of sex. This novel came out very easily, almost naturally, like a part of me lives in the violent-cunt world of Razor Wire Pubic Hair. Not sure, maybe part of me really does. Parts of me are all over the place. But I believe this world is an ugly/beautiful one to live in, I think I love it/hate it. Perhaps you will too.

Also included are 34 portraits of women living inside of this razor world. Women who are not in this story but have lives very similar to Celsia's. Perhaps some of them are friends of hers, or neighbors. Perhaps some of them are dead, killed off by rapists or zombies. It is difficult to tell. I only have their images to give you.

The other day I had a dream that I was married to a sliced-up dead girl, like the one in the remake of 13 Ghosts. My girlfriend says she wanted that to be her dream. She wants to go inside of my head, so we can have a threesome. This is how I spend my time.

- Carlton Mellick III, 3/17/03 3:22 am

"Traditionally the woman is virtuous, but during the rainy season their sexuality is stimulated by the environment. You can sense this oozing feeling inside, which is like the movements of a snake."
                    - Shinya Tsukamoto

"Technology wants to be in our bodies."
                    - David Cronenberg

This book is for me. I wrote it. It's mine.

Act One:

My Life as
Multi-Sexed
Fuck Merchandise

SCENE ONE

Lime-flavored tattoo on the back of her neck as she tells me, "You're going to give me a baby."

The metal of her eyes click, goo-white film over black orbs, old dog eyes, her smile a cluster of purple poison thorns. And arms slender locust-like when she pulls me out of my home, my coffin/drawer on the side of a sky-caressed building, a red-womb where I've lived in half conscious dreams of multi-lives for the past six years, being fed through meaty tubes controlled by women workers within.

The rubbery female chains me to her steel clothes/armor and walks me out of the wet-wasteland of city, hands around the sandy hip, tiny body over-powering my body.

"You're much thinner than the others," the woman says to me, a wheel-squeak voice. "I like them weak and more feminine like you."

I'm not all feminine, I argue with my eyebrows.

A raspy giggle, "I love girly fuck toys."

girl 01

SCENE TWO

"We must hurry through," the woman pierce-whispers to me, rubbing a metal hook-like fingernail against a breast and penis head. "The rapists will be out soon. The wastelands are infested with them."

Rapists? my nipples ask.

"Barbaric and sex-crazed, corrupted by a nymphomaniac disease. They mutilate and fuck every living and non-living thing they come across."

My bare feet go crunchy through the crab-textured landscape, howls around me, intense nerves under my skin.

"Don't worry, we'll be there sooner than later," she tells me. "Just don't slow down. The rapists are behind us."

girl 02

SCENE THREE

She strings me from the ceiling of her living room and removes all my fresh plastic wrapping.

"Here is your new home," she tells me, smiling and licking her face with a sticky dragon tongue, rattle-stepping into the next room to remove her metal clothing and limb attachments, stripping off the clank-materials. And she returns brushing cobweb strings from her arms and presents her cute/sickly flesh to me. Her skin paper-pale from wearing heavy clothes too regularly. Thick metals, chains, leather, her skin rarely exposed to what is left of the sun. Ropes and plastics sewn through her leg and arm meat as if some kind of fashion style.

I know the importance of fashion styles.

The woman circles in her stringy nakedness, cutting into me with sharp eyeballs.

"I promise not to kill you first," she says. "I normally wear my hook-nails when mating and get fast-

fast excited, I just can't stop cutting." Her head cocks. "They just don't survive long enough to . . ." Eyes click. "I'll make sure it doesn't happen with you. I bought you for mating . . . not just pleasure purposes."

I'm too weak for you right now, I tell her with my fingernails, body swaying in the nerve-openness.

"You're not used to being disconnected from your container."

I should eat first.

Dipping her poison tongue and she says, "After I plug you in, you should forget about hunger and weakness."

My teeth whimper, *I hope I am satisfactory.*

"Yes, yes," replies the woman, massaging an enthusiastic breast. "I want you to last for a second child."

Is that possible?

"It happens," the woman circles to my back and shuffles mechanical trinkets in a box, and I shiver uncomfortable.

You are very beautiful, shaky-telling the woman, but she only answers with more shuffling. *The other females who considered purchasing me were not as high quality as you are.*

"Don't call me *high quality*," she says. "I am above merchandise." Then plugs a cold metallic rod into my excretion shaft and flips the power on. It drives a claw of electrical waves into my body, up my ass, erecting my two members to full extent, the skin ready to pop and peel, hardening my nipples, my vagina hairs standing up into needles, spiky and tickling.

It's not that bad, my voice now panic-harsh and gyrating, gasping lungs.

"What is?" asks the woman.

Being merchandise.

"Maybe for you it is satisfactory, you are part male," she comes to me, eyes twisting under pasty film, "But a woman is too free-spirited to be controlled. There is nothing that can hold us."

What controls a man?

The electricity begins to purr into my ears.

The woman rubs her faded nipples into erection. "His penis, of course," grabbing one of my solid members. "They lived, they loved, for sex. Slave to cunts. That's why they are extinct. Only women and flesh-creations such as yourself can live in today's society."

When I was in the testing period, I enjoyed drawing, I say. *It is what made my artistic rating so high. If I were not a manufactured product for women, I would have lived for art rather than sex.*

"As long as you have a penis and testicles attached to your body, you will live for sex."

No, sex is not that important to me. Sex is just a game to play. A game adults can have fun with.

"You are a fuck toy, created for sexual purposes," says the woman. "Sex is the world to you."

No, there is more to the world than sex.

"Then let me cut off your man parts," drawing a blade razor from a flesh pocket in her wrist, bringing it underneath me. "If I remove them you will become like a woman. I will allow you to live in my home freely for the rest of your natural life, free to draw and paint."

Are you sincere? I ask, gentle-green.

"Yes," clicking her eyelids, "I am sincere."

You don't care that you will lose money on me?

"I am sincere."

I stare at my penis and testicles, and then my other penis and other testicles, they are painfully stimulated, cringe-crawling. The vagina and breasts would be so lonely without them.

SCENE FOUR

I say, *But don't you want children from me?*

"Of course I do," she responds.

Don't you want to mate with me?

"I've purchased you for this purpose."

Then why would you do such a thing? Why would you abandon me?

"I'm giving you a choice between freedom and sex."

But I thought you wanted to mate with me! I thought you wanted me to be your fuck toy!

She calms me by rubbing my upper penis. "So you'd rather not be free?"

No, it's not that ... I would rather not disappoint you. You are so beautiful that I'd do anything to please you. You deserve a child, not a sister.

The woman smiles hook teeth at me, her man-like product, and pulls shiny objects from a box, shaking her head in a crude *slave to cunts* way.

Are you happy? I ask.

"I am happy," replies the woman.

SCENE FIVE

The woman connects wires to her nipples, plugging herself into the wall to saturate the electric-sting juice, vibrations deep inside her, between flaps of skin, and attaches herself to my body . . .

Tube tendons like snakes of meat creep from her arms and ribs, sliding into my chest, into veins, ripping open flesh and suctioning into place . . .

The woman contorts herself, turns her legs into ropes to wrap around me as she pumps . . .

Tubes emerging from her stomach absorb the nutrients from my body, sucking them into her, to feed her egg. My nerves raw-shivering with the electricity, nerve-jerking. I can feel the strength flowing from my muscles.

Her pulsating breaks whines from my mouth as her sucking tubes dissolve/eat parts of me. Her eyes swallowing me, opening her mouth wide to stretch her jaw as she comes, over-over again — the electricity forcing us into climax with every motion and it feels so painfully alive, yellow-sparkling, licking my teeth at the thought of my body being eaten to feed her future baby.

She continues contort-curling around my torso, wrapping our bodies squeeze-together, forming a meat ball, hanging from the ceiling, gyrating, oozing puddles onto the floor, sweat puddles that reflect our shivering mass back up to us, swinging in slurpy echoes . . .

SCENE SIX

Awaking with only sick flesh remaining on my body. The woman staring coldly at me as I prickle-groan, staring through a mirror from across the room, admiring her colorless naked reflection.

She cut me down to sleep on the rug, my skin extra sensitive to the wicker-wool fabric.

"I'll order a meal for you before your trip to the recycling machine," says the woman.

My eyes dazing across the carpet landscape, *I thought you were going to save me for a second child?*

She applies metal hook-jewelry to her face and leaves the room, her belly swollen with all my nutrients.

A spider crawls across my face and nestles into my nostril for warmth. Too weak to wipe it away, but strong enough to crack a smile as it scratches an itch deep down inside of my nose.

girl 03

SCENE SEVEN

Above the table there is a lamp:

It is a fleshy globe radiating dim light, pulse-shifting, breathing awkwardly as it spins like a tiny planet or moon, pump-moaning at me. From inside, hands press outward against the globe's skin, twisting fingernails trying to break free, a mouth kissing against it to make an outline of teeth and tongue, reaching out to me to give a kiss.

Exposing naked breasts over plates of food, sitting at the table below, I am discovering two lovers are trapped within the lamp, the dangling skin balloon, stuck together with nothing to do but fuck themselves away, the insides surely pooled with thick juices for them to soak in, a soup of nutrients and chemicals designed to keep them healthy and fierce. Sex as lighting for the room.

My owner clicks into view, the carpet cringing underneath her feet, squishing, nude moon-skin with metal sweat. The light-lovers in the glowing/shifting ball emanate brilliance onto her shiny sweat skin.

"You're not eating," says the woman, demon eyes curling around my neck.

I don't understand food, I tell her, a finger pressed into a mound of mush.

The woman cocks her head. "Yes, you're used to being fed by machines."

I glance down at my plate: an assortment of greasy structures, lumpy tubes and strings of muscle tissue thin as hairs, perhaps made from discarded sex merchandise like myself, processed in the recycling machine to feed women.

My penis becomes a rising tower, poking into the splintery wood of the table, at the thought of becoming food for the women, to be chewed, soaked in their saliva, rolled between cheek and tongue, lips hugging me, sucked on for flavor, imagining the slide down a female throat to become a bulge in their pale-fleshed bellies. Dissolve, melt inside of them, my meat being absorbed into their warm muscle, rushing through their bloodstreams to taste every quiver of their bodies.

The woman sees my penis rubbing against the wooden table and grabs hold of the head, squeezes it hard and red, her eyes staring demon-black and her mouth open wide enough to swallow me. She squeezes powerful, grinds my penis head against the splintery wood, my lungs shifting to scream but pause in sick-tasting. She wants to see me cry. I do not cry. But I push my head harder into the wood, and the woman scrapes it back and forth, tick-shocks of burn, blood deciding to dribble out of the hole.

I jerk, whip the penis away while holding back the other, showing her the drops of blood issuing out of the hole.

"You don't have the right to resist me," says the woman, reclaiming the penis from me. And she grabs an intestine from my plate of food, wrapping my wrist against the chair's arm, tying the slime-rope tight against the dust-cold metal. She groans out of her nipples, cuts me with her hook-nail fingers in a caress, takes a new intestine-cord from the plate and wraps it around my chest, stretching the meat-rope to the back of the chair and curling around my ankles, stealing the balance from me, awkward-sitting helpless. And the woman goes on the tabletop, squatting position, leaning over to me, her skin's metal shining my eyes blank.

"I'll feed you," says the woman, crawling her fingers through the plate of meats, sponging her digits deep inside, the warm flesh of a recycled sex toy, possibly one that she owned before I took his/her place. She finds a long slab and strokes it with the soft side of her palm, grips firmly, lifts it to her neck, creamy chest, perking her nipples like knives that point at me, stabbing the air to get to me, and she takes the meat to her mouth and licks it from butt to tip, closes her tricky lips around one end. Then slides it deep inside her mouth cavern, lifts her chin and begins to swallow it whole like a snake, a large bulge in her neck as it is forced down to her stomach sack. And when she finishes, her tongue sighs a lengthy lick, eyes falling to me as if I'm next.

"Your next," she says to me.

I can't swallow like that.

"I'll have to feed you like a baby then."

A handful of stringy meat, she squishes and fills her vagina, stuffs it deep and dangling from the sides. And she sits her spine against the corner of the table, wrapping spider legs around my neck. Arches her back to rise her flesh-bowl to my purple lips.

"Eat it from me. I'll keep it warm and moist."

Then she squeezes her thighs, cramming my face into her cunt, squirting some of the meat into me, fat grease oozing from her to paint my throat and breasts. The taste startling strong, meat probing under my tongue, stimulating virgin tastebuds, so sensitive it overwhelms me with flavor.

And slowly, I scoop into her with my black-goo tongue, licking the food out of her to eat and the woman wiggles, tiny whines growling out of her, vibrating as I dig for nourishment to replenish my brittle structure, begin sucking to draw it all out, and the woman twitches at me. She grabs hold of my skull and digs her razor-nails into my scalp to put me deeper between her legs, grinding me into her crotch, attempting to swallow my face whole like she did the slab of meat.

Soon, my tongue can't move because she's squeezing against my face so rough, can hardly breathe, and she fucks my face. Grinding into my upper lip bloody, my teeth scraping against a tangy switch, until her whole body quivers and my penis explodes bloody cum into the splintery table, flowing agony onto my thigh, into my vagina crack.

The woman is lying in the scatterings of my food, slowing her breaths, grease still flowing down her icy thighs, running down my chin.

She eventually separates us and leaves the room to bathe.

"I'll keep you a little longer," she mumbles in the distance, not too concerned that her words are hardly audible.

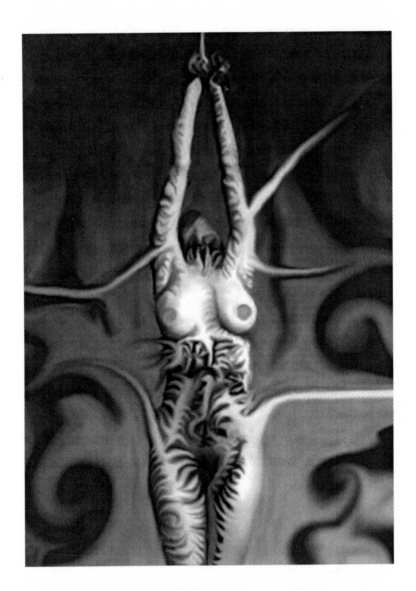

girl 04

SCENE EIGHT

The woman is staring at me, examining, just learning the details of my structure.

"You need a name," she says, licking the metal rings in her upper lip.

I want to name myself.

And my words convey a flick of hook-nail slice, an itchy blood line across my cheek, mad at my wanting to name myself or mad that I spoke without her permission, my eyes shuddering downwards.

"My sister should be arriving soon," says the woman, polishing metal knives on a piece of leather and cloth. "She is going to decorate you for me, so that your skin isn't so plain and embarrassing."

Embarrassing?

"Blank skin is dull. Being the owner of a plain-fleshed fuck toy would be death to my reputation as a warrior." Rubbing my naked breast. "A slave is a canvas made of skin."

girl 05, girl 06

SCENE NINE

When her sister arrives, a wave of pin-emotions cricks into my neck, my vagina curling indoors, digits graze threatened, covering shaded cheek skins, peering sharply with awkward eyelashes at me, beyond me.

The woman is very tall, long ropes of hair that end in iron hooks or spikes, nails growing out of her skull flesh, and she doesn't wear much clothing or any armor as my owner woman, just belts and chains randomly wrapped around her, her skin is much darker and sun-weathered than my woman's. And the sister has two extra pairs of arms, and tattoos of vaginas covering her body like oversized pores. She resembles a spider, spiky-dangerous.

And she also has razor wire pubic hair, and when she smiles a shiver rips up and down my back muscles.

"That's him?" she asks, a scratchy whisper, her face coiling up.

"Yes," says the woman. "That's *it*."

"He's scrawny," says the sister, folding her pairs of arms, "and neither penis is anything special."

"I like it enough."

"But what about when I want to borrow him?"

"It's not for you," says the woman.

The woman, still walking nude, pours a jug of strong battery liquors into three cups. She creeps one to me and whispers a tickle-tongue to my ear, "It's going to be painful."

I choke down the contents of the cup, a relaxation wave. The sister puts me on a leash, so tight it hurts to swallow.

SCENE TEN

The Sister takes me up some rickety stairs, tiny crabs pinching my toes. A salty liquid sweating out of the ceiling kisses my face and slips under my lips to hide.

The living room mutates, scrambles my mind and familiarity, drives me into believing it is a vast canyon landscape now. A valley of trees and mountain peaks made from the tables and chairs, tiny spiders and beetles now look like bears and oxen wandering the hills.

The woman does not follow us, staying below to become part of the canyon. I see her as a river and waterfall, reattaching metal armor to her body parts to make splashing noises. Her eyes folding back into her head and tongue licking her nose, a jumping-snake from the river . . .

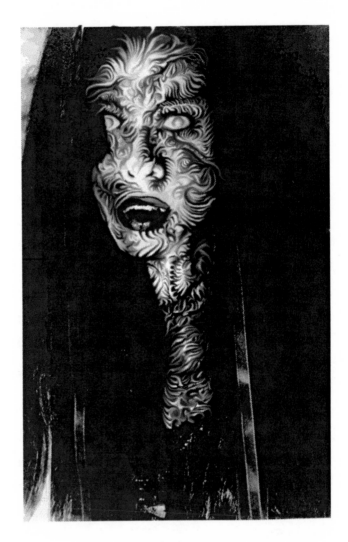

girl 07

SCENE ELEVEN

I find myself in a garden-like room, soil and plants on the ground, spider webs glistening in corners, vines crawling the wall, arching, trembling.

The Sister throws me hard against the wet-dirt floor, goes to a shelf hidden amongst black roses, the razor wire slicing against her inner thighs as she walks, light bulbs dangling from the ceiling moist with electrical fluid.

"So what's your name?" asks the Sister.

I haven't been named.

"Well," says the Sister, "Celsia will probably name you after herself. She always does that with her pets."

The Sister takes her tools from the shelf, long thin blades and hooks, plus an assortment of metal rings and studs.

"Raise your arms," the Sister orders.

Slowly submitting . . .

Goatskin cuffs wrap tight around my wrists and I find myself pulled out of the seated position.

"This won't be totally pleasant," says the Sister. "But be thankful. Most fuck toys rarely get designs as nice as the ones I'm about to give you. Only Celsia and I hold fuck merchandise to high esteem, especially after I make them beautiful."

The Sister uses the hook-like instrument, attached to a black fluid container, and approaches to illustrate my surface.

"Not to mention," the Sister continues, "Celsia happens to be a prominent warrior on this side of the wastelands. You should feel honored. She's fought off seven hordes of rapists so far, that's four more than any warrior living today."

I squeeze my eyes shut when she comes to me, her scent strong enough to make me dizzy, a vagina smell. It grows stronger, fondles my nose hairs as she fills her tools with electricity and touches it to my stomach. The tool vibrates slime into me, ripping slowly as she paints, my eyes trickling with awkward soreness.

When I open my eyes, I see what radiates her strong scent. The sister's vagina tattoos that cover her body are not tattoos at all, but real cunts, all over her, not just in her crotch. On her arms and legs, her thighs, many on her back and torso, one between her breasts as if the breasts were its buttocks, some on her shoulders, her neck, a small one behind an ear, and one on her forehead so that she can get her brains fucked out.

And they are breathing, dripping onto my skin as she cuts me, and I breathe in her green-ant smell, closing my eyes again, the cutting of my flesh quivering my thin remains of muscle, fists aclench, twitchy in the eyes.

The Sister finishes the stomach tattoo — a pattern of hands layered on hands layered on hands — and moves on to tattoo inky beetles on my breasts and a penis.

Hands on me like leathery puppets.

This penis is very tender from its last encounter with the splintered table and the ink gun pierces right into the soft spots, cutting up to the head until the penis extends, hardens to give her a more suitable canvas to work with. I go into jerks as the needle hits nerves, muddle-whispers shower out of my lips, Sister's lips curling a smile. She grips my member and braces it against her thigh, just next to an unnatural vagina.

And sensing its presence, a wet tunnel, as if steam was rising from it, droplets of moisture condensing against the head, the needle spasm-cuts designs into me, teeth engine-grinding.

The Sister's thigh moves upward, dripping the back end of my head just slightly to saturate it, and her juices soothe my wounds.

Staring out over her brown-freckled shoulder to watch the vines creeping the wall . . .

The Sister flexes her leg muscles rapidly so that her thigh can fuck my bleeding cock, and another vagina snatches up my second cock like snake's prey, rubbing against a clitoris, greasing the penis slicker, and the tattoo wounds begin to sting as her motions quicken.

The needle cuts me closer to her hole, attempting to pierce through to her insides, and it strikes my penis head. A muscle spasm in the limbs, tightening ass, tears cutting my eyes.

The Sister finishes and smiles fangs at me, hanging dirty, and she bends down to lick the trail of blood running from the tattoo.

My owner woman, Celsia, stomps a spider in the entrance and her stomping makes the Sister jump back, wiping my blood innocently from her lips.

"Is it done?" Celsia asks.

"Not yet," answers the Sister.

"You'll have to finish another time then. I'm going to take it to the underground."

"Already?" asks the Sister.

"I want to show it off," Celsia responds.

SCENE TWELVE

The woman, Celsia, leashes me with a veined and fleshy rope. It squeezes around my neck and makes sweat dribble. My clothing consisting of barbed wire and belts pissed on, gently around my shoulders and waist, with a chainmail loin cloth.

The woman wears a new metal suit, made to expose her white breasts in an upheaving manner, her nipples clamped with steel and linked together with thin chains. She has horns curved and slick, penis-shaped and have certainly been used during enthusiastic masturbation.

Celsia decided to pierce metal cylinders through the flesh on my neck and behind an ear, making parts shine for her, so that we would match for the evening.

The Sister peering down into the landscape of living room from the staircase, watching us through the spiny decorations.

Celsia opens the carpeting and leads me down

underneath her home. There is a wet tunnel down there, blue-smooth and warm, we walk deep into it, feet squishing in muscular puddles. Lights are fluttering us, snake-like machines with large heads swim through the moist atmosphere of the tunnel, brightening our path with their hypnotic motions.

The walls of the tunnel twitch as we step through, a tight passage, my wire strap grating against its soft walls, sometimes cutting blood. And Celsia's palm smoothing it caressing its tender bulges as she walks.

"Your name is Celsia 2," she tells me.

Celsia 2?

"I'm naming you after myself."

The space between us and the walls becomes thinner, thinner, until we have to shove ourselves through sideways, probing through the agile meat. But our spiky attire is ticklish, and the walls flex together, squeezing us so firmly we begin to slide, force-slipping through the greasy passage like food swallowed down a long throat, deep down inside of the earth . . .

SCENE THIRTEEN

We pop out into an open arena of women and their sex merchandise. There are so many of high decoration, similar to Celsia, dark and leathered and metal-ridden, all with razor wire instead of pubic hair. They have sex toys leashed to flesh-ropes, some with more than one pet. They are all engaged in some sort of violent orgy, ticks and crab-men crawling surfaces. Wet and fleshy emotions leaking out of them, creeping all the way over to me.

"You can interact with the other fuck toys," Celsia tells me, unleashing me. "But you are not allowed to speak," pushing me into the center of the arena.

She decides not to play, only a watcher standing with other watchers, three women with silver-painted skin.

Four fuck toys surround me, squatting low to the ground and blinking fiercely as if to communicate.

All different sexually, some with two vaginas, some with arm-sized cocks, some with six breasts, some with multiple-mouths. None of them claiming one gender or the other, but most of them similar to men, dripping with masculinity. Especially one particular sex toy in front of me, whose muscles could break my head in orgasm, but this sex toy has only a vagina and not one penis, nor any breasts. It acts as the leader, shifting from side to side with gorilla limbs. And the others mock him/her, shifting from side to side, long cocks dangle-swinging in their shifts, and I'm confused about what they want, scared of the sweat and smells.

They want to watch us screw each other, the leader whispers to me.

My confused expression does not disperse.

The glowing snake-lights are whipping behind us, scattering us with shadows, investigating, curling the warm air around us.

The fuck toys are sweating and hardening, all of them much larger than myself, tight muscles, only the strong ones are kept as pets while the weak — other than myself — are recycled into meals. These vagina-bearing men, one even bearded, working their bodies all day in the arena to please their female domineers. Approaching me like wolves, on all fours, their eyes stabbing at me. I try to step away, but my muscles are weak from mating with Celsia.

They catch me without difficulty, swiping me off the slick-meat ground, cheering from the crowd of women — half-absorbed in conversation, half-absorbed in the orgy.

The others tie my hands to a post in the center of the arena. My ankles cuffed together around the other side.

"Celsia 2, are you making friends?" Celsia yells from across the flesh field.

I open my mouth to reply, but one fuck toy shoves four fingers inside, holding down my tongue.

It/he says, *Don't answer. She just wants an excuse to whip you in front of her friends.*

Removing the fingers, *It's her job to whip me.*

You're speaking as if you don't want freedom.

I was offered freedom, but decided against it.

The others cock their heads.

Celsia yells, "It's time for the hoota beast!"

Then the other fuck toys clear my front, gathering behind me. They squeeze my shoulders and want me to relax.

Don't worry, they say. *It's not that dangerous.*

The women begin to chant: "Hoota beast, hoota beast, hoota beast!"

Coming from the shadows: A tall woman, thin with limbs twice the size of mine, like a stick woman, approaching sharp-clawed with a leashed animal behind her.

"Hoota beast, hoota beast, hoota beast, hoota beast!"

The leashed animal is half the size of a female, a blubbery ball of skin, dripping as it moves, the strong ones behind me, hands jittering on my shoulders, bracing me for its arrival. Multiple gopping eyes, six on each side, front and center a large slit, sliming, lick-noises, bubbling.

"Hoota beast, hoota beast, hoota beast, hoota beast!"

It is a giant vagina with legs, spiky hair on its top and around the sides.

The stick woman ghoul-smiling, her eyes sparkling wet with the light-snakes whipping behind her ears, teeth showing excitement, gesturing her pet closer to me.

The hoota beast's lips swell upon arrival, obedient to the stick woman, walking up to me to do its job, warmth against my upper thighs, breath coming out of the slit.

Celsia's watching with a curled lip, digging a hooknail into her belly button.

And the hoota beast encases my lower region, its moisture cloying me, itchy-close to one of my cocks.

The strongmen cluttering behind, tin-rustling noises. They slip away my protection, my cloth, the shell of skull on my forehead, the extra skin from my genitals. Pulling tightly on the barbed wire straps to dig into the scuff, my chest stinging, emotions of orange-frustration overwhelms me.

The stings ride my nerves down to the penis, rising it involuntarily into the great canal of the hoota beast, vagina beast, encompassing it, swallowing me whole. Inside, it is like a mouth with extra thick saliva and six fat tongues massaging in fuck-like waves.

Celsia has a proud smirk on her face, watching the creature screw me, center stage of the arena, her friends with amused smirks at me as well, clapping metal gloves for my shivering performance. Their razor wire pubic hair makes clinkery noises as they clap. Cheering for the scared and weak little fuck toy, getting its first hoota beast love, saying *cute cute*.

And the orange-frustrations rise higher and higher inside of me, ready to pop, as I see Celsia digging a shiny finger deep between her thighs.

girl 08

SCENE FOURTEEN

I awake one morning on a pile of human hands, holding me up like a bed.

Dozens of palms open against my skin, finger-shiftings that massage in parts, tickle in others, engaging flaps of skin.

My memory seems a bit confused, blotched, as if weeks of my life have suddenly disappeared. I cannot recall being placed upon a bed of living hands, not even entering the room in which I come from sleep.

The hands move and my back skin stretches for a burn-pain that clouds with irritation, sometimes skin pinches between fingers, crushes against a bone.

Shock-jerks, a quiver. And two fingers are probing into my vagina, rubbing until the walls seep strawberry goo. A penis hardens, and another hand snatches it up like a child to candy. And then another hand finds my unrisen member, fondling it to make it equally firm, a fingernail crawling up the shaft. It goes balloon-expanding. It goes solid, almost too far, skin ready to burst, and the harder it gets the deeper the nail digs into it, my spine riding the pain.

When I try to move, to see where I am, where the hands come from, they pull me back down, seize my wrists and ankles to keep me there, choking the back of my neck.

Many hours and stages of fatigue and skin abrasions . . .

"Friendly, aren't they?" Celsia's voice echoing through the chamber.

I don't see her anywhere. The hands hold me in such a way so that my eyes fixate a brick wall that reaches up to a ceilingless sky — green and red cloud atmosphere.

Celsia's face emerges from the corner of my sight to dominate my vision, her metal decorations squirming in and out of her flesh reflecting the green and red light, smile sharp teeth.

"I usually lie on this bed for hours. Shall I lie with you?"

I prefer to get off, please.

Celsia's face shifting happy to sour, a hook across my chest as she bends down to turn a lever on the floor. The hands melt into goo and dribble off my flesh, out of my vagina, and my body lowers, finds itself on a cold plastic-wrap table.

A drop of blood slips between my breasts and Celsia bends down to lick, her eyes glaring at me like iron marbles.

girl 09

SCENE FIFTEEN

Celsia, walking naked through the kitchen, has recently been decorated with razor wire in her crotch, ruining her soft vagina with the violent metal pubic hair her sister and friends have displayed publicly.

And the Sister has been working her insecty designs all over me as well, mostly during my unconscious periods. Some mornings I'll wake with a new aluminum strand through my lower lip, another woven into my breast meat. Sometimes I wake with a tender black painting across my arm or belly. Sometimes my skin cut and laminated green so that I appear to have fish scales on my neck and ribs.

"The acid clouds have moved over the wasteland again," Celsia says to the Sister. "We won't be able to cross for months."

"That means more rapists near town."

"Enough to overpower us if they want."

girl 10

SCENE SIXTEEN

Celsia never noticed the people that live in the attic.

They stay up there hiding from her, never coming out not even to play black tarantula. I hear them moaning sometimes, weeping for a place outside of the attic, looking for things on the inside that they cannot find. Their relationship with the house must be an old one, residing long before Celsia claimed it for her sex games. Her arrival must have scared them into hiding. It's so sad to be them, poor people in the attic in the darkness hiding all the time, scared of Celsia's razor wire pubic hair, scared she will cut them with it.

They must not have been loved by her or perhaps her presence is intimidating and crab-like, perhaps they are sex products such as myself, perhaps scared of the real world, scared of growing old, dying, getting raped. Locked themselves away from reality, living in the darkness to make their heads more clear, crying out at times when the darkness overwhelms them, makes them feel lost inside their own heads.

SCENE SEVENTEEN

It is raining drops of spiders over the rose bushes and fig trees this morning, slow motion from the tar clouds as they come down on sticky threads. I watch from a window, my neck leashed to the wall, a hand sliding down my shoulder and cutting scratchy lines to my breast.

"There are zombies beyond the garden," Celsia tells me.

She points to motion among shiny bushes in the distance, but there aren't any walking dead I can see.

"They're sad creatures," cutting the backside of my ear. "Wandering aimlessly for something they'll never find. Wandering until they are too rotten tomove anymore."

Do they attack you?

Celsia shrugs her puffy white lips. "It disturbs them to see me so close to them. I am a reminder of what they can never have."

What can they never have?

Celsia slides a blade or perhaps a finger between my legs, down the crack of my ass.

"Sex, of course," she responds. "What else could they want?"

SCENE EIGHTEEN

Dirty-cold with sweat afternoon:

The Sister is making me put my hands in her cunts while she continues to mutilate my body with metal designs and blood piercings. I am beginning to look like one of them, studded ring on my clit. Like a woman. But I have a penis with a hook through it.

The woman, Celsia, is squatting naked over a large machine made of flesh, a gigantic mouth wrapped around her waist, slurp-sucking something bloody out of her pubic region.

Smack to my face, noticing my hands have stopped moving inside the cunts, the Sister screaming, "Pay attention. She's only depositing her womb into the incubator."

I was only watching.

"She doesn't like it when you watch her," squeezing my hands hard against her for an angry groan. "I swear you fuck toys are more trouble than you're worth."

girl 11

SCENE NINETEEN

It only takes a couple hours before the incubator finishes its job, the machine gurgling in the corner like
Celsia's washing device and cooking device and recycling device, rumbling in the corner to process her
womb into a child, squishy bubbling noises echo the
fortress.

When the child is done, steam rises out of the
flesh machine and makes a whistle noise, a human
whistle screaming from the same lips that were wrapped
around Celsia's crotch. And both Celsia and the Sister
run to the oven with metal aprons on.

Turn away, look back to the garden to maybe
spot the hiding zombies.

But the reflection in the glass:

Celsia is behind my shoulder, excitedly holding
up a monstrous child to me with knife-teeth smilings.
Its deformed features and bubbly parts squirm in its
mother's claws, a trickle of blood whenever one of her

hooknails catches a pinch of flesh.

What is it?

Celsia cringes, "It's our baby!"

She turns the child away from me, pressing it to her pasty nipple. "I know she doesn't seem human, but it's your fault. *You* are the father!"

"No," the Sister enters, stepping to the child and dripping cunt-sweat onto its bubble-chest, "it's a monster because your incubator's old and rusty. I told you to get a new one."

"It's not a monster!" Celsia hollers at her leaky sister. "All babies look this way!"

The Sister smears her juice on the baby like oil, staring into its bulgy black eyeballs.

Turning dizzy-gazed, I examine the machine the infant came from. It is large enough to contain dozens of babies, filled with wires and meat, plugged into the wall. A hole centers, dripping with food and slime, crunchy hair surrounding the soggy opening, bleeding, trembling, waiting to be sewn up.

"Look," the Sister says, "it's smiling."

"It is a flesh-bag," Celsia comments. "But still a beautiful one."

"Yes," says the Sister, "Like a fancy purse!"

SCENE TWENTY

At times, Celsia hits me for no apparent reason. She gets red-faced and just strikes out, hits my knuckles with a hammer to make the skin curl away. And she doesn't even care about her new baby lying crooked on the table.

I'm raw inside, my cunt feels like sandpaper meat on the walls, crunchy knives coming out. Spiders appear on me sometimes to eat scabs from me, take pieces of my neck.

Sometimes Celsia gets mad at the sun for never shining and runs outside, throws a hammer into the air at it. But it never flies higher than a dozen feet before falling, a thud on the ground sending particles of green and orange dust into clouds.

She doesn't touch her razor wire pubic hair at all during the orange-frustration moments. As if it is not as intense to touch anymore. She treats it like grass or normal head hair instead of sharp flesh-slicing metal that her nerves — and mine — usually quiver to. Even the deepest cuts on the inside of her thighs aren't enough to excite her.

On these days, the people in the attic speak in whispers in the shape of rose bushes, thorns hooking into my brain, cutting delicately along the veiny lines clustered amongst the plump tubes under skull.

Celsia doesn't seem to hear them, as if her brain has been washed of their sound, even when they hit high pitches her ears do not rise or twitch like mine, ignoring them until they are numb-nothingness to her.

She is bleeding on the ground, resting her legs from her bush, her tender parts open to the tangy air. If she calls me over, I know it's because she wants a painful fuck, sex as a weapon.

SCENE TWENTY-ONE

The Sister does acrobats on the ceiling. She calls it her exercises, but doesn't tell me how she gets up there and doesn't fall. The melty baby lies on the floor underneath and doesn't say anything or do anything. It just sits there and complains about how ugly it is.

When the Sister sweats, it drips like rain onto my dinner plate and onto the wiggling baby/thing, the vaginas covering her body become soggy for my services, penetrating eyes at me as she bends backwards, folding herself into halves.

Celsia doesn't know the Sister uses me at night, sneaking fucks there and here, and the Sister makes me keep it a secret. She knows Celsia wouldn't let her waste my energy on anyone without her presence.

Right now, Celsia is on the roof, making sure the rapists do not attack. She has been afraid of them ever since the baby was born. The rapists move like wolves, searching for things to fuck and eat, sometimes

fucking and eating each other if they have to, but raping strangers is much more fun than incest.

The Sister bridges her back to drip vagina juices
onto my forehead, into my eyes, and when I glance up
she bursts laughter. Then grabs my arms, pulls me up
into her web, tucking my body firmly between her legs
to hold me quiet and prisoner.

SCENE TWENTY-TWO

I don't like the baby. It just sits there and collects greasy spots, makes a home for hungry insects that want to tunnel through its limbs. All the healthy meat was ripped off of my body to feed this sack of jiggle-flesh. Such a waste of my self. I am in pain at nights because of my sacrifice to this child and it does not thank me ever. It doesn't even have the decency to stop being so deformed and ugly.

It's like the bloated blubber of a drowned pig with eyes, hands, a foot, and a soggy black mouthhole covered in hair. And it never wants to play black tarantula or spot zombies in the garden. It just complains and complains, sometimes sleeps or sucks on Celsia's tits, which oftentimes makes me jealous.

Why did Celsia purchase my body to make children if this is the type of product we would bring into the world? How can it expect to ever be loved by anyone, even its parents, when it looks so ugly? If all babies came out this way, no childhood would ever work out right, nor any adulthood.

The world would be all illness.

I am made from illness.

Act Two:

Something Living Inside of Cunts

girl 12

SCENE ONE

"The rapists have taken the village," says a fishy bald
girl at the door, teeth chipped spicy with sores in her
eyes, speaking lightning words, a breast dangling out a
tear in her brown-bloody shirt. "It was a massacre of
sex. They fucked and fucked and fucked, raped everyone to death with knives."

"Are they headed this way?" Celsia asks.

"I don't know. I ran and ran and ran."

"Get inside with me," Celsia ripping the tiny
woman out of the outside, peaking the distance then
closing the door.

"Watch them," Celsia tells her Sister who curls
down from the ceiling. "I'm going to warn the council." And she straps spiky armor to her shoulders and
disappears out the door, too quickly to think of shut-
ting it behind her.

The Sister gone from the room already, bored,
gone to practice tattoo-art on the blubber-ball of child.

Wind knocking the door against the side of the house as it enters, knocking, slamming/knocking. And from my chains I watch the young woman shivering, eyes-locked at the open doorway, haunted landscape trying to creep inside, drool fizzing down her chin to puddle between her nervous breasts, teeth clenched, her bald head stained with sticky liquid. I crawl her pulsing parts with my sight, intrigued by a woman who is actually weaker than me, could be dominated by me. And then she catches me staring at her and stares back until I look away, and then she eyes me up and down, sees my cocks hard and red.

SCENE TWO

"Get off!" Celsia screams, slapping the girl on top of me. And the young woman slides off of my chest, off my penis and scrambles across the floor.

"Bitch!" screams Celsia, kicking her away from me, our bodies shiny with sweat and other thick fluids. "It is my fuck toy, mine to fuck!"

The tiny girl curls up under the table, my blood running out of her mouth from when she bit into my shoulder, bulge of sun-fried belly jiggling from rapid-breaths, cowering her eyes so that Celsia won't hit her again.

The Sister entering, long hair sticking to her chest vaginas.

"You were supposed to watch them!" Celsia spits at her.

"I was busy taking care of your baby, as you call it," says the Sister, and Celsia throws herself onto a stack of dirty furs. She calms, tells the Sister, "The council is only putting up a barricade around the center of town, which means they're leaving everyone else vulnerable, especially us."

"What are we going to do?" asks the Sister.

"Try to protect ourselves," Celsia says, silver mushrooms sprouting from the corners of her eyes. "The best we can."

SCENE THREE

Just before she drilled a fingernail in my butthole, that young girl had told me, "I am Tamu," my toes writhing beneath her.

She kept her eyes closed when she fucked me, imagining me to be something else — the Sister enjoys to do this as well — pretending I was male. The girl wouldn't go near my female parts. Pussy sauce boiling out of me, but she would not lick or even touch it. She called out a man's name when she fucked me, crying sometimes or laughing out loud, afraid of the rapists coming to the door. So many emotions for such a tiny person. There was even the emotion called *happy*, which spilled out of her just before Celsia came into the room to beat us.

The girl is still hiding under the table, even though it is morning and the morning-bugs swirl her face, crawl up and down her mud-sticky limbs. Too scared to masturbate herself awake, as Celsia and the

Sister did earlier in the morning. Crying, ugly with fear. I smile at her but it was awkward and my lips become itchy, so I scratch my smile and begin to think about windmill blades.

SCENE FOUR

The Sister is dancing naked in the garden with the undead, grinding feet into the earth and rubbing steam bodies, while Celsia puts up spiky bars around the perimeter of the house.

Moving in twisty curls, the Sister delirium-dancing, whipping her hair, the long braids hooking zombie meat sometimes, and she splashes them when her body-cunts begin to drizzle. I still cannot see them, I see only their presence. I see bushes shifting sometimes, and from the shadows hear growlings when the Sister gets too close to one of them. They cry out in green-anger, because their cocks are too withered to fuck her. And they also cry out from fear of the rapists in the village, anxious-stampering to get inside the barricade, begging for sanctuary.

I can see Tamu across the room, hiding, stuck under the table as if she were tied there, as I am tied here, far from my reach. She's still crying, her eyes tight together. Shoving her breasts in my direction with every outburst of air, as if she wants me to touch them from across the room. Her dirty body shivering from fright or from lack of sex, lack of a man's body.

I am similar to a man.

SCENE FIVE

Outside during Celsia's break, stepping through icy mud grass crabs with thorns attacking my toenails, watching her frolic excitedly. All thoughts of the approaching rapists separated from her head and whooshing behind.

Celsia cuts down a chokon tree in the fortress cemetery and empties its meaty center onto the spidery pavement. She smiles in a horrid way, dirty teeth from eating spice roots, waving to me to come let her fuck me in it.

The wound on my leg is getting crusty and worms are eating the rotten parts, but Celsia won't let me swat them away. She drools on them, watches them devour tiny pieces of me. Her nails are always stabbing, creeping my breasts. Her tongue is friendly/sharp, selfishly probing.

"Come, come," Celsia tells me, and I step carefully through the prickle-mud to get to her, my nudity shivering nipples hard, bumpy.

She enters the trunk of the chokon tree, slips into its lips, twisty roots curling around the sides. And when I arrive to its pulse-opening, the oozing scent overwhelming me dizzy, Celsia snatches my arm in her claw, pulls me deep inside to darkness, to warm meat and fluids, heating me like a womb. And Celsia fucks slowly, absorbing the tree's energy, and my energy, shifting up and down through the trunk's tunnel, pretending we are a giant penis pumping this long friendly cavity.

SCENE SIX

By nightfall, the barricade is finished and Celsia can rest. Too tired to even fuck, she goes to stand on the roof of her rust-metal castle, towering over the nail-textured fields and tar-red sunset. Her razor wire pubic hair raised high for all to see, glistening on her shivery skin against the dim war-lighting, fires on the horizon, an armless woman masturbating in the road with her toes, legs curled inward, broken so that they can reach her sex hole.

The Sister is greased up rot-sweaty from dancing with corpses. Her dirty wetness sliming over the many vaginas that populate her body, two of which have yeast infections at this moment, eyes focused on the quivering road for sign of the rapists.

I watch from inside, spying through a hole in the ceiling. They have left Tuma unguarded and the tiny girl, still beneath the table, looks like she has plans to dart out from hiding, capture me, take me under there with her, rub her cunt all over me. But she hesitates. The women might see her from the hole in the ceiling and then feed her to the rapists.

The two sisters are up there all night, battle-ready, touching each other to keep warm, to keep them excited to kill, to satisfy them sexually, hook nails creeping pale scummy flesh, wet flesh. It is dangerous to be horny with the rapists around.

They sleep up there together also, close as they were in their mother's guts, bathing in mind pools. Celsia picking green snails from her legs and giving them to her Sister for a Christmas present, and the Sister throws them over the side to pop on the ground, stinky water seeping into the asphalt.

Sometimes there are worms in the sewer eating brains away from rapists and the living dead, sometimes they get into my brain and dance around. But Celsia is strong. They never get into her brain. Her armor has spikes and razor-sharp knives. She stares black-eyed at the moon as it smears into the color black. She sleeps against her sister, and the Sister sleeps against her.

The night goes on for days and not even the rapists can do anything to stop it.

SCENE SEVEN

The other day Celsia told me about how they used to breed dogs with windmill blades, creating a sort of spinning/teethy creature with a violent urge to bite at the wind, barking and squeaking.

They must still be around somewhere, barking through tunnels in the ground, eating scraps from the people living in the under world, their garbage or maybe even bits of their limbs.

Sometimes Celsia hears dogs growling in the fields nearby, or whimpering, perhaps they are memories of the time when people claimed pets out of nature. Perhaps they are looking for a way back into homes, hoping their windmill blade features will not send their masters screaming. Perhaps the dogs now prefer their wind to Man. The wind is much stronger, much more important. Something to look up to.

When the windmills/dogs are fucking, you can hear their orgasms through the trees. You can hear them in everything, on the particles carried by wind, and if you're lucky you can see them spreading their legs in the cold dirt, waiting for the wind to penetrate them.

SCENE EIGHT

The rapists have yet to come and the nights are crawling like rubber smoke, so slowly and not letting us get any sleep, barbed tension, ugly mops dizzy in the cellar.

On cold days, one or two of us runs from the fortress to the abandoned section of town for supplies and food, knowing the rapists can never handle the cold. They bury themselves deep underground, wrapping their bodies into warmth, making sure the cold doesn't make their sex organs shrink.

Today is the Sister's day to go for food, and — decided by Celsia — I'll be brought along for exercise. I've been getting flab-soggy, Celsia says. And nobody wants that.

girl 13

SCENE NINE

Outside, the world is frozen.

Everything is cold and hushed. Only the wind crawls in the blue-scented moonlight.

There is a twat-frog hopping down the road beside us. The Sister watches—pubic razor wires make slice-clashing sounds as she walks—the frog's plump hairy body jiggling as it goes. The rapists love to eat twat frogs—twats with legs, they've been called, miniature hoota beasts.

The rapists must be close to have them on the run. Normally they are in holes hiding from rapists and from little girls who might want to stick dildos or twigs into them.

Little girls are so cruel to small animals with vaginas.

girl 14

SCENE TEN

We stop at an aviary of glassy birds manufactured to tweet and bounce upon plastic branches, shimmering in the cold morning. The audio boxes on their necks have deteriorated, making their chirps a gargle-sputtering that echoes the paper hills.

The Sister hides us here for a break, stepping deep into the frosty pond where our reflections come out clearer than reality. She had no idea she could look so clean, amazed at herself and touching her parts to see if it is really her and not some other vagina-covered woman starring back at her.

Seaweed clothes dangle off her shoulders, salty-flavored. The glass birds hopping from branch to branch.

I can see her breath dripping out of her, icicles want to form from her wet holes. When she pulls me to the glassy floor to fuck me, her holes warm me up, even her razor wire heats the skin as it rips the under section of my belly. But afterwards, her juices soaking my body begin to freeze in the wind, giving me shivers, like fucking her had given me an illness. And her sickness has a smell that crawls through me like blood, and I want to go back home to Celsia and fuck inside of chokon trees . . .

SCENE ELEVEN

Her eyes averting, the Sister pulls me along the road until we get to the town. We get there. My nerves chill-sharp. The barricade is a gigantic hollowed out centipede, stories-stories high, curled so that its mouth kisses its tail, encompassing all of the town. So mighty and purple-powerful to the eyes, but it's actually not much for protection. One could easily just crawl between the centipede's legs and enter the town.

So we crawl under the legs of the giant beast/barricade and find emptiness, empty except for a few glass snakes and wooden feet. The whole town disappeared, sucked into the earth.

We see the other side of the centipede far off in the distance, hovering out of the mist. And the wind carries a whipping sound, it whips red lines across my back legs, torso, neck.

It makes both of us feel alone.

girl 15

SCENE TWELVE

Walking back in hunger, failed mission, so alone inside and out.

The Sister stops us in the middle of the road to put tiny versions of Jesus Christ inside of her cunts. She just loves to feel them inside of her, wiggling around. You can find them crucified on the flowers all along the path.

I watch her as she runs excitedly through the field, snatching the Christs out of the flowers and stuffing them head first down the cunts, and she keeps grabbing them until every vagina has one under its lips.

Sometimes the vaginas swallow him, digest him. Sometimes they spit him back out, mutilated and covered in goo. We continue to walk and I hear one or two crying in a slight muffled way, the Sister with a BIG smile on her face. She is no longer alone inside.

girl 16

SCENE THIRTEEN

It's all darkness as we return, night squeezing its legs
around us. The moon aches.

  We smell dinner in a far off place . . .

girl 17

SCENE FOURTEEN

"Rapists came and gone," Tuma says from a butthole window above the threshold.

Inside, Celsia confirms the information with a nervous nodding, flickering fingers at us, pointing to four dead bodies hanging from the ceiling in the living room, blood dripping from headless necks, drying into a film on their coarse tits.

"I fought them off," Celsia tells us, "but they'll be back with more in the morning."

"What are we going to do?" Tuma asks, curled up behind my legs.

"Let them come," Celsia says.

The Sister nods, noting, "And we'll rape them back."

girl 18

SCENE FIFTEEN

Morning comes and Celsia works violently, setting up
another fence around her home. She has removed her
metal skin and is now sweaty-greased in her stringy
underclothes, her white body a blemish in the red-
speckled field.

The Sister is again dancing with the dead in the
garden, but this time she is slow-dancing, embracing
them against her slippy skin with her eyes closed loosely.
The gray-orange sky beats against them as if on purpose.

You can tell the dead are falling in love with her,
she cradles them in her arms, reminds them of what
they have been searching for.

Tuma hasn't spoken a word today, she hasn't
thought to put on her clothes. I tell her she'll infect a
sickness, but she just doesn't give in . . . lifting my legs
to lose herself on my pleasure parts, as I tell her a bed-
time story.

girl 19, girl 20

SCENE SIXTEEN

Tuma has a pet that she has been keeping between her breasts. A pet slug/hand/jellyfish creature that can melt flat as paper and form around the girl's young breasts. Sometimes she wears the pet as a shirt, lets it coat her torso, a flat rubber-fit, so tight that she'll appear naked when stepping through greasy-black sections of Celsia's home.

Her breasts are like the creature's cage—two pointy guards holding it hostage. When the creature —whose name is *Muggy Tim*—wiggles without her permission, Tuma will flex her breasts together and crush discipline into the gelatine pet. But Tuma loves Muggy Tim for its warm affection and feeding it is easy because it eats the bacteria off of her body, never needing to take baths ever again.

Tuma is not afraid of the rapists anymore. They don't seem to be coming. It has been days and they have not returned.

"We scared them off for good," she says and smiles as Muggy Tim cleans the inside of her thighs.

SCENE SEVENTEEN

The Sister has been sneaking zombies in one by one over the past few days. She does it at night when Celsia is on a sex break from triple-barricading the fortress and climbs on top of me and sometimes brings Tuma and Muggy Tim into the mix, embracing us in her sharp teeth.

The zombies have been hiding from us in the cold dark corners and between the walls. I can hear their rustling, moaning, sometimes they call to me, try to entice me to come and find them. To eat me? fuck me?

I can smell their rotten stink when I step through corridors, shreds of their skin lying in hallways, ground into the carpet fabrics, peeling like a snake.

Tuma and I wonder what the Sister gets up to in her bedroom, what she lets the living dead do to her. Does she take them into her bed with her? Tuma quickly nods at me, giggling and petting her Muggy

Tim on her breasts.

SCENE EIGHTEEN

The first time I came in direct contact with a zombie was when I was going to the bathroom one morning. Celsia was setting up another wall outside and the Sister was teaching Tuma how to masturbate with acupuncture needles.

The zombie was a woman, with her face rotting in such a way it looked to be melting off her head, rusty liquid dripping from her neck and eyes.

It did not speak to me, taking a bath in a scum pond of sweaty house-fluid which she must have mistaken for bathtub water. I tried not to make any sudden movements in the slime woman's presence. I pissed through all of my urinary tracks at once.

girl 21, girl 22

SCENE NINETEEN

Celsia dances naked with God when everyone else is asleep. I hear noises from my room sometimes and wander out and see her there in the living room.

She prays to Him to leave Heaven and come down to Earth to be with her. She wets her crotch and moans between prayers until God has no choice but to come down and dance.

He does not fuck her, because that would be incest. Celsia, as all naturally born children, is a child of God. But being strangely attracted to Celsia's sick and violently seductive appearance, God comes down to dance with her every night when no one else is looking.

He sometimes hums to her, pressing His sunburnt chest against white tattooed mounds, and Celsia would cut him with her hook-nails, digging into his back like dirt—the measurement of how far she digs into one's flesh is the measurement of how much she loves that someone, or how much she wants to fuck them.

Sometimes she sees me watching and calls me out to dance with them. Gods might not be able to fuck their children, but it is perfectly legal and natural to fuck their children's creations. So Celsia strings me from her living room ceiling and watches grinning as God licks the space between my tits.

I try not to look into His eyes when He enters me, digs into my cunt. The power so strong inside that it hurts my eyes black. I stare past his shoulder, watching Celsia watch me as she masturbates with long spiky tools. And when God comes inside of me, it makes my whole body shake volcano-like. But He does not give me an orgasm. He has to go back into the cunt with His tongue and rub it all around, feeling emasculated for failing to bring His sex-opponent to climax, that long white beard rubbing against my asshole, a giant hand groping a cock and a breast.

It takes so long.

Celsia is so much better at giving me sex.

I love her so much more than God.

SCENE TWENTY

I'm dreaming that the sun is infected with cancer and the light it emanates is blacks and dark orange, making colors knotty and twisted.

A woman without arms and legs is dreaming this dream with me. She has a mat of hair on her chest and begs me to fuck her, does not *tell* me to, she whines, cries for me to. Her flesh burnt-colored, with the sun overhead, shadow particles crawling up her foresty breasts.

She melts to fuzz when I am not looking. In the corner of my eyes I see her dribble to liquid so that tiny animals can drink her flesh/sauce, and then returns to solid when my sight jerks to her direction. She smiles, fluffing her hairy chest, exhilarated.

Please, please, please, she calls to me.

She rubs her carpety bosom against mine, itches the penis resting between them. *Take me the way you want to*, says the legless/armless woman, *make me your fuck toy.*

Outside of my dream, Celsia is getting angry. She peers over the dream as if we are in a goldfish bowl, swimming naked through the wet. And I hold the woman's pubic hair chest close to me, caressing it quickly before I am awake. But Celsia does not wake me, smiles razor-fangs, veins cracking out of her forehead and cunt.

She plunges her metal fingers into my dream, my mind/goldfish bowl, spinning her hand around until she snatches the dream woman from me, pulling her out of the dream, squeezing, hooking deep into her sex hair until it soaks her fingers red. And she drops the body back in my brain, sinking to the pebbles and treasure chest on the bottom, blood clouding in the water.

Then Celsia wakes me to give me her black-eyed stare.

"How could you do this to me?" she cries, smacking my cheek bloody, rips at my hair.

It was just a dream, I tell her.

But she has left the room in a shrieking rage, blood droplets streaming down from my forehead.

SCENE TWENTY-ONE

The house is sad today. The zombies walking through its hallways are like bacteria, making it puke-sick and depression coated. A dark foam is rising out of the underground, probably from the sex arena, overflowing with cum and sweat and blood. The people down there fucking so much until the place overflowed with sex-juice and drowned them in it.

Beetle men crawl down the walls of the house like tears, scattering out of the windows/eyes and dripping down the brick and metal interior, piling up in the corners with crick-churky noises, singing.

Celsia hasn't fucked me in days. It's making me nervous, I think there is something wrong with her. The Sister says that Celsia doesn't want the rapists to smell our sex from the landscape and follow their noses to us, but I think she is just pretending. Something is wrong with Celsia, something is wrong with anyone who doesn't want to have sex.

My erections are constant most of the day. I am mentally stable. The Sister has tiny skeletons of Jesus Christ inside some of her cunts and they tickle her in the right way. She keeps some of his skulls in a porcelain jar and urinates on them when she has nothing else to do, squats over them and marinates them, shows them who is in control.

The house is getting colder as the days go on this way, its sickness contaminating us, making us see things that aren't real. It seems there's nothing left in the world other than sex. It seems it has always been this way.

SCENE TWENTY-TWO

Tuma's delicate young brains are scattered all over the balcony pavement this morning, leaking from bars and tree fingers.

I am staring at her right now. Wire spiders scattered throughout the sausage-texture, filling shiny bellies. The look on her face is one of loneliness and exhaustion. Hands soft open-palmed against the iciness breeze.

We take the ugly mops out of the cellar, ones hiding in the cracky corners, filled with beetle men and webs. The mops sweep through the brains, scoop through Tuma's wicked thoughts and dirty dreams, talking in whispers to her spirit lost in the stringy brain tissue, the spiders climb the trunk and eat the mop beetles, eating so much they puke insect shell and brain sap.

"She was so beautiful," says the Sister, but Celsia twists a metal clamp on her nipple and bites her lip.

I try not to look at her face as I clean the brains, looking out into the wind cutting through the desert, barbed wire fields, dogs barking in the fields with their legs spread outways.

Her body is absorbed into the flesh of the fortress, placed into a dark meat cabinet in the kitchen and dissolved into nutrients to feed the walls, ceiling, oven, vacuum, fireplace . . .

SCENE TWENTY-THREE

The baby/thing is still alive.

I thought Celsia put it to death days ago, but she has just been hiding it from me and her sister, knowing we want it dead. Its crying can be heard at night echoing through the shadows and creeper vines. Waking the zombies to shift between rooms in search of it, to quiet the little creature inside their jaws.

Celsia is in hiding as well, it seems. Sometimes I hear her on the roof or scurrying the barricade outside, but I haven't been in her presence since Tuma died. She only haunts us, gives us glimpses of her, lives like a ghost.

I am stepping through the kitchen now, my feet sticky to the tile, silence so loud it makes my eyes bleed. The Sister is here, eating some mushy food which was recycled from Tuma's flesh, smiling and rubbing her belly at me, petting the warm Tuma meat inside of her.

"Come and eat some of her," the Sister tells me.

"She's so tasty."

I shake my head.

"She's absolutely delicious," the Sister says, rubbing some of the meat goo on her breasts, huff-moaning with her eyes slightly fastened as she polishes the nipples, thinking of Tuma, her young flesh rubbing against the Sister's breasts.

I creep across the floor and pour some meat-goo into a bag to eat, the flesh smooth and tender, caressing the inside of my body, slithering down my throat.

I think she's the best food I've ever eaten.

SCENE TWENTY-FOUR

Now I can't find the Sister.

I can't hear the giggling/moaning, I can't smell her cunts anywhere, that aroma that saturates entire rooms in her presence. Gone.

Like Celsia, she must be hiding in the fortress somewhere, leaving me alone with the living dead creepers, cunt-ripping fingers sneaking inside me when I'm not looking and then disappearing when I open my eyes, rotten meat smells stained into the floor, onto my tits, my cock.

Stepping through darkness halls, distant baby cries, insects talk to me from everywhere. I don't know how to use electricity, so there is only one light illuminating the fortress, a small yellow bulb next to the greasy bath tub in the kitchen, making it uneasy to explore too deeply into the hallways.

I sit down in some sticky fluids, draw a picture on the ground. Waiting for someone to take care of me.

SCENE TWENTY-FIVE

A day goes by.

I'm still alone, twisting my nipples and masturbating with forks, staring down at my cunt, my cunt wide open staring back at me, something crawling twitching inside of there. And something crawls in the room with me, Tuma's pet snail-jellyfish-trumpet, taking to the carpeting, slitherings, burns a blood-scab wound onto its belly a bath of milk and squid fat rubbing into the carpet fibers, across the room.

"Where are the others?" I ask the pet, but it continues across the carpeting, into the kitchen, into the machine Celsia's baby came out of, to return to the womb and never come back out.

Outside, there is a rumbling wind, rumbling-rumbling-rumbling, growling too, rumble-growling. And it grows louder but I'm not quite sure what it is, where it comes from. Outside, it is cold and blank. Nothing is there but rumble-growling, which can not be seen.

Something is coming this way from over the hills.
I feel alone no longer.
I want to be alone again.

SCENE TWENTY-SIX

A couple hours pass and the rumble-growling fades, but I am not quite sure why how what. And the outside is too dark for me to see now, the light bulb in the room glaring the window when I try to look through. I'm blind to whatever it was that rumble-growled but it is not blind to me.

Upon the wall, the wall straight ahead from where I've been sitting for hours at a time, I see shifting and dripping. My head jerks to see it there—though I am unsure whether it has just now appeared or if it has always been there and I've never had the chance to notice—a giant cunt, much bigger than mine, much bigger than Celsia's or any of the cunts on the Sister's flesh. It's as big as a doorway, just pulsating/dripping there on the wall, breathing deeply and quivering at me.

My hands can't stop themselves, they pull me up to its lips, go right inside. Smooth-oozing along the inner walls and the edge of its plastic-flesh mouth, a rising of scented steam warming the space between my breasts. It is like the giant cunt is calling me to fuck it. My arms traveling deeper inside, up to the shoulders so that my breasts and mouth can rub against its squirmy affection.

And then I feel my legs go in without my permission. Stepping inside, until my whole lower half is bathing within the giant cunt, and it begins to fuck me. The wall begins shifting around me, fucking my body and I try to fuck back but I am so small and weak compared to it.

It frantic-fucks me, plunges me deeper inside of it, up to my chest to my waist, to my chest to my waist, to my face to my chest, to my face to my chest, gasping for air, rubbing my breasts and cocks against its wet sides, until the cunt swallows me whole, squeezing its lips together to suck me deep inside, cumming all around me, spastic orgasm like it is trying to break me in half, but it stops moving, breathing deeply. Its walls still pressing me deep inside, holding me in here like a prisoner.

SCENE TWENTY-SEVEN

Eventually the giant vagina gets irritated and spits my body out onto the kitchen floor, my meat soggy and covered with goo-slime, and my warm sticky coating turns freezing cold once the draft hits, squatting down into a ball to warm my breasts with my knees.

girl 23

SCENE TWENTY-EIGHT

From the other room I hear a rolling sound, marbles rolling across concrete, and then I see them. Eight or nine milk-white marbles rolling in my direction, some as large as grapefruit some as small as grapes.

No, they are more like eyeballs. They have pupils and veins in them. Once they arrive to my sitting position, they move their pupils in my direction. Eyeing me up and down, eyeing my cunt, sniffing it with their nerve clusters.

And then most of the eyeballs move away from me, scurry across the floor and into the giant cunt on the wall, and disappearing inside.

Two little ones have decided on staying by my feet, glancing at my vagina and then at my eyes and then at my vagina, like a puppy.

From inside the slit on the wall, I see the eyeballs peering out at me, observing. And then the giant vagina curls its lips into the shape of a mouth and begins to speak.

"You are a dildo," says the giant cunt.

I don't know what to say, watching the eyeballs in the cunt stare at me spider-like.

The giant cunt continues, "You were manufactured for sex, a fuck toy, like a dildo. You are just a dildo that can walk and talk."

I have a soul, I tell the giant cunt.

"You are just a dildo that can walk and talk and possess a soul," says the giant cunt. "But a soul is not all too significant a feature to possess."

What is a significant feature? I ask the giant cunt.

"A cunt," says the giant cunt.

SCENE TWENTY-NINE

Who are you? I ask the giant cunt.

"I am The Something That Lives Inside of Cunts," says the giant cunt. "I live inside of all cunts, including yours."

And I look down at my cunt to notice the two tiny eyeballs at my feet have managed to sneak by my legs and into my vagina, now staring out of it at me.

"I am the closest thing you have to a god."

I don't understand, I tell the giant cunt, not looking it in the eyes.

"A dildo rarely understands," says the giant cunt. "The only thing a dildo understands, or *needs* to understand, is sex."

But what about a soul? I ask the giant cunt.

"A soul was created to make sex more exciting," says the giant cunt.

When I was being manufactured, I was told that sex was invented for reproduction, I tell the giant cunt.

"No," replies the giant cunt. "It is backwards. Reproduction was invented for sex, to make sex more constructive."

What about Heaven? I ask the giant cunt.

"Heaven is where a bunch of angels live," says the giant cunt. "Angels are creepy old men who masturbate all day long, watching human beings have sex. The world is their pornography."

I thought it was paradise, I say to the giant cunt.

"Only on orgy days," says the giant cunt. "Or whenever God has sex with you."

God fucks me, I say to the giant cunt.

"It was divine, wasn't it?" asks the giant cunt.

I prefer Celsia, I tell the giant cunt.

SCENE THIRTY

Crashing-banging breaks the quiet in halves.

Smashing sounds from outside trying to get in, a whole army of crashings. They are trying to get through the barricade outside, to get to me, to fuck me.

The rapists have come, I tell the giant cunt.

"Oh, good-good," says the giant cunt.

Aren't you scared? I ask the giant cunt. *They will rape you to death.*

"Embrace the rapists," says the giant cunt. "They are my children."

I don't like them, I cry to the giant cunt.

"They bring bliss to a dildo like you," says the giant cunt. "A violent orgy of cunts and fucking."

I hear the crying outside, whining for me to let them in. The rapists growling like a metal-tornado, ripping down the barricade, ripping down the walls.

"I am not a dildo," I tell the giant cunt.

girl 24

SCENE THIRTY-ONE

Rushing through the darkness of hallway, I've got to find Celsia and tell her about the rapists, tell her to fight them away, save me from their violent cunts and knives.

It takes most of the evening traveling through darkness places, only lighting comes from a paper moon dangling outside of certain windows, glowing eyes in certain twists of the hallway.

The living dead have done well turning Celsia's fortress into their home. Every room I come upon in search of Her is a scene of necro-eroticism, living dead women touching each other ripping each other's meat apart.

In one room I find a giant moon-glistening spiderweb with several zombies trapped on it like flies, and from the ceiling there is the Sister playing black tarantula hanging from a shiny string to catch the undead ones curl them into her breast to suck crispy blood from them. And I notice that the web is not made like a spider's. It is made of razor wire, the shiny metal ripping through zombie flesh, the web attached to her like it is an extension of her razor wire pubic hair, and the strands are emerging out of the Sister's cunt like it would a spider's lower abdomen cutting the vaginal lips on the way out, wrapping around a zombie to cocoon it in her pubic hair.

SCENE THIRTY-TWO

I find Celsia cradling Herself in the darkest corner of
the fortress, on the darkest floor. I had to crawl under
a bed through an air vent over a mountain of broken
tables and chairs to get to Her. She's sitting here staring at the blankest wall she could find, naked cold flesh.
   The rapists are here, I tell Her.
   She nods and chews a finger.
   I sit next to her, shivering, hoping she will lean
against me to warm us but she shows no sign of movement. Our child, the bag of soggy meat, is over there
in a pile of dead blankets and rats, I'm staring at it in
disgust and scratching a nipple. It has been tossed aside
like an old ugly purse, lying there in sickly breaths.
   "I've been waiting for it to die," Celsia tells me,
glances cold fish at me. "I haven't fed it for days, hoping it will die, but it keeps breathing and crying."
   The rapists are coming, I tell Celsia and She nods.
   "I knew the baby would die. Babies always die.

I just wanted to have a child for a while, a beautiful child. Just to see what a baby of my flesh would look like."

We need to fight them off, I tell Celsia and She nods.

"But the child came out a freak. My flesh must be sick to produce such a monster. I want it to die so I never have to look at it again."

I don't want to get raped. I tell Celsia and She smirks.

She stands and stretches her icy white skin.

"You were born to get raped," She tells me, her teeth sharp and leering.

SCENE THIRTY-THREE

We can hear the rapists breaking indoors, flooding in soupy screaming and fucking everything in the kitchen, finding zombies and beating them to the ground with their fierce cunts, pubic hair grinding undead lips off their faces.

Celsia does not want to hide. She takes me out of the dark side of the fortress and tells me to wait in the middle of the hallway for them. She has me stand there naked, rubbing my cocks until they are ready for the rapist's drooling holes. And She crude-chuckles at me, a whimper under Her breath, razor teeth biting Her lip bloody.

"You were born to be raped," She says, locking herself inside a nearby bedroom.

Act Three:

Quality Time with
Rapists and Zombies

SCENE ONE

The rapists are full of sex and lazing about the fortress, not planning on killing us or leaving us or fucking us at this moment, just resting on us in tatters. Our blood mixing with their diseases, their scabby cunts, scabby cum. And the zombies have been torn to shreds, their flesh-pieces scattered throughout the home, parts/limbs have torn off inside of cunts inside of buttholes, mouths, teeth marks all over my body, bites taken out of me.

The slime lady's head is deep in a meaty hole in the wall, sinking. Her expressions slightly disappointed as she blinks, slips down farther, farther, farther.

One of my cocks has been ripped off of me, from my chest, ripped off when being fucked by some steam engine cunt, her razor wire slicing it free as she went thunder-cumming, blood oozing from her mouth my mouth pooling onto both our bellies, onto our brains, smearing sticky flavor between us. The penis flopping onto the floor, discarded.

But I don't feel pain, as if the penis were made of toenail or wartskin. The hole where it had been no longer bleeds, the scab almost invisible, healed up easier than a nosebleed.

I step through the collapsed sleeping rapists covered in glory, sometimes waking up to pull me to the ground for a quick screw then back to sleep, searching for Celsia but finding only fuck after fuck.

Getting to the stairs and climbing above the mob-painted room, to the hallways which are now lit by glowing snakes from the underground, twisting and curling cocks of light.

SCENE TWO

The Sister is in a back room raping the rapists.

She has them in her web, her razor wire pubic hair. A long cord from her central vagina encases one of them, holding it from movement.

Then she starts reeling it to her, pulling the wire back inside her cunt like she is no longer a spider but a frog with a long razor wire tongue, cunt now a frog mouth. And the fly is still a fly, now waiting to be swallowed rather than sucked on, the Sister's lips stretching six times their width, wrapping around the rapist, gulping it slowly inside of her.

She spots me in the doorway, a seductive stare at me, black smiles as she takes the rapist inside up to its waist legs dangling cutting against the razor wire. Her eyes now glossy and colorless, gleaming at me trying to trance me. And I see into the cunt on her forehead, see into her mind, she is imagining that I am entering her cunt/mouth instead of the rapist, swallowing me whole. As soon as the prey has been squeezed completely within, the Sister licks her facial lips with a black snake tongue, licking her vaginal lips with a razor wire tongue.

A giant bulge in her belly, the rapist curled up inside, quickly dissolving. The mound making the Sister's body twice its size, but soon it sinks, soon it is a much smaller bulge, soon back to a flat metal-scaled stomach. And the Sister continues her seductive trance on me, slithering to me with her legs spread apart, razor wire emerging from the crotch, smiling zombie-eyed at me.

But I am not hard for her. I am looking for Celsia. She is the only one allowed to swallow me whole with her cunt.

My body away from the Sister, into the sex-scented darkness, hearing the Sister enter the hallway much more metal-scaled, hunting for someone else to feed her cunt.

SCENE THREE

There is nothing left outside.

When looking out of the window, there is only blank darkness like someone painted the outside of the windows black. And it is not because the night is without a moon, it is because there is nothing left outside of this fortress. Only a colorless blank. Everything that once was the rest of the world is now collapsed from our perception.

I go out the front and it is blank, empty of textures and colors. Only the sound of an angry breeze smacking against the outside of the fortress. I do not dare take a step outside of the fortress, I fear that I too will become a part of the blankness, where all of my senses go numb.

Staring out of the window, I do not even see my reflection in the glass.

girl 25

SCENE FOUR

I am guessing time has stopped.

Since there is no longer such a thing as a sun or earth, we have no idea how to calculate time, no real use for clocks. And it seems to take so long going from one side of the fortress to the other. The Rapists throwing me down and fucking me whenever they get the chance. I don't find her for maybe a day, a week. She is on the feathery side of the fortress where all the long blankets hang, all the rapists infecting this area are too exhausted to rape, lying on the floor with moans and fizzle-cries.

I find Celsia right in the center of the half-dazed rapists. She is missing her arms and legs. And looking around, many of the laze-rapists are without limbs as well, arms and legs scattered throughout the dim flyingsnake-light.

What has happened? I ask Her.

Her voice crooked and distant, face moving to

my direction, head balancing on its neck to speak to me, I took the halfroff.

"The halfroff," Celsia explains, "is a sexually transmitted poison. Those inflicted with it fall apart limb from limb. It is fatal once the head falls from the neck."

My confused look does not fall from my face.

"I want them all to die," Celsia tells me.

My face cocked at her, leaning over her cunt to warm my cheek.

"And I want you to kill them, I'll give you the poison and you will act as a carrier, it will not slant you as quickly because you are not natural, you will fuck them apart, fuck their arms and legs off. Fuck them to show them I am stronger than they are. I am so strong."

SCENE FIVE

She wants to fuck me one last time, fuck me for fun
and give me the poison, but she has no arms or legs.
She tries crawling on top of me, shifting her waist from
side to side, but she just rolls off onto the floor. Her
head bangs against itself and orange-emotions break
into paper-machete-emotions.

And she says: *Rape me.*

What are those words? They came out of her
torso, so weakly and soft.

Make love to me, she says.

Yet again, there are her words, such pathetic
words that make her so less attractive to me. Women
are supposed to be aggressive and domineering, not
delicate and tender like a fuck toy.

"I will fuck you to death," I tell her, the words
awkward from my mouth, but Celsia smiles as if they
are what she wanted to hear.

I don't know how to overpower-fuck someone,

but I have little time to learn. I know how to fuck, I have been a spectator of fucking, I have watched others fuck me in this way.

I bring my shank to her opening, my only penis left, curl the head near her razor wire pubic hair, looking into her old dog eyes, so sad, twitchy.

Please-please-please, she says to me between whines, and I spit blood between her tits.

My penis rock hard into her before she knows what to think, rip through her razor wire pubic hair like weeds, rip them out of their roots with my cock, plow them down, my cock hammer-ramming through her with sharp teeth, screaming at her, my cunt sealed up sewn lips shut, ignoring my tits as the bounce with my barreling body, fucking and howling, fucking, crying, in tears when I fuck her head off rolling from her neck into a pile of arms and legs, still fucking her torso, just stare at her tits, those tits and this cunt are all I need to cum, she wants me, I need to cum inside her.

SCENE SIX

It's not difficult to spread the poison to all of them, draping myself over the darkness, over the table, over the baby-making machine, over parts of zombies, and all the rapists within view just hop on top of my cock and tits, their gnatty twisted cunts bee-swarming all around me, biting my skin with rusty pubic hair. Machine-animal-spit-groans from their vicious cunt mouths.

It took so many fucks to get them all in, not sure how many I did, enough to spread the poison to those who fuck the most the ones who will transfer it to everyone else.

There is a leader of rapists, the horniest of them, they made her their leader because she fucked like a tank, fucked more than any of them. She was the one with the wide nipples whiter than any other flesh on her body, the one with the red crunchy hair tangle-knotted into strips, she's naturally blonde you can tell by the roots, but somebody made her fire red somebody sat on her head and let menstrual blood flow down her forehead her neck, dying her hair with life.

She is taking a liking to me, she comes to me more than all the others, fucks and fucks, I make sure to come inside of her, make sure she gets the poison deep in her blood so she can spread it to all her sisters all the sticky bodies that clutter our tomb, tomb of fucking.

SCENE SEVEN

"Our tomb is erotic," the blood-haired rapist says to me, lying next to me in the crab-calm darkness. Because she is a rapist, her words come out rat-twisty and curled.

She has me wrapped up in her sisters, mud and cum sticking us together, cocooned.

"We are trapped inside a giant cunt or giant testicle maybe," the blood-haired rapist says. "Nothing to do but feed our desires, pile into a big sticky ball and fuck each other to death."

We go for a walk in the darkness, the dried scum building between our tits, holding my ass. Most of the rapists around us have fallen apart, lying half-dead in piles. No blood escapes their severed limbs as if they were born armless legless like the limbs were just plastic attachments which have happened to melt away.

"Moans echoing from them all," says the blood-haired rapist. "They are helpless, perfect for raping."

The women clutter the floor screaming to be fucked, raising their cunts in our direction, begging us to lick them fondle them love them quickly before their eyeballs fall out of their heads, when they can't even rape us with their eyes.

"Fuck them," the rapist leader pushing at me her vicious screams her old cunt-smell sweeping across my body. "Fuck them!"

All their bodies in pieces on the ground, all of them without limbs, awaiting my cock or cunt, their leader crying, snatching my member to grow it hard my sex tools are not working right. She sticks a finger in my ass and squirms it hard, but it breaks off inside before it causes any erection, cupping her mouth on the hole to suck it out but it is too deep. I feel it digging through my intestines trying to make its way up my throat.

She screams, gets on her knees, fucks one of her limbless sisters with a strapped-on knife, cock-shaped blade, yelling at me, "Fuck them, fuck them, fuck them."

And the crowd of halfed rapists scream in harmony with her, "Fuck me, fuck me, fuck me."

And the blood-haired woman shrieks as she fucks the rapist with her knife, the knife handle digging inside her own fuckhole, rubbing agony in the tender places. And when her victim dies, she does not stop knife-fucking.

"Fuck me, fuck me, fuck me."

And as the rapist goes faster on the handle of her knife, stabbing her dead sister, an arm breaks off to the floor. She doesn't stop. Fucking with her eyes looking at her brain. And the other falls, plops on the ground. She slows, close to orgasm, whining, blood pooling around her knees.

And then her legs give away, breaking off at the thigh, throwing her onto a pile of dead rapists, jerking her head back against the wall, against the giant cunt still part of the wall. The jerk so powerful it knocks her head off her neck, rolling it into the giant vagina lips, sinking, sinking it deep into its dark blank hole.

And with that, the rapists go silent. They lie there, letting their eyes drop out of their sockets, letting their brains go loose from their skulls, letting their tits drift off their chests . . .

Their cunts sliding out of their crotches . . .

girl 26

SCENE EIGHT

I'm all alone now. In the tomb. Even the glowing snakes have been infected with the poison, falling to the floor to fade away.

I have to light the hair of a dead rapist on fire to see my way, light their hair with the stove and use their dissembled heads as my lanterns, light the hair in their mouths and their entire head lights up like jack-o-lantern, glowing orange skin. Searching to accomplish something before my limbs detach from me . . .

There are moans ahead, up over there beyond eyesight. Rapists who must still be half-alive and losing their limbs.

No, wait. Not them. The rapists have all died. This moaning is not coming from them, they are coming from the attic, from the people in the attic. The sad ones who live in the shadows.

"Who are you?" I call to the people in the attic, bold cockroach-air against my buttocks, red noises vibrating, listening.

girl 27

SCENE NINE

The attic is up a rope ladder in the dungeon. You have to go to the lowest level of the fortress to get to the uppermost level, take a rope ladder up a chimney/tunnel to get there.

I climb it with splinter-itches against my greased palms, my lantern/head dangling over my shoulder. But even with the lantern, the darkness is so strong, blackness all over you, I can feel its weight on my skin, a hand packaged firmly around me.

They are silent of moaning when I arrive to them, but I can sense old echoes of their moans still resonating in the corners. I direct the lantern to them, to see their faces. I want to speak to find out why they cry so much.

However, the light reveals nothing alive, the floor mostly bare besides sawdust and old nails.

But:

"There you are . . ." I say to them once I see the

walls.

The walls: covered in human-sized photographs of *men.* Real men, not man-like screwing toys. Naked men, strong and smiling, a whole crowd of them plastered in all directions of the room, all of them staring at me with their square heads.

In the center of the room there is a single object.

A penis.

A penis as large as my arm, lying on the floor, dried and stuffed.

The frozen images of masculinity just continue their stares/smiles, staring at my breasts or are they trying to glance secretly at the giant member at their feet? Wishing somebody, some woman or vagina-like thing, will come along, pick it up, give it a good caress and worship it like a god. Or maybe they want me to worship them as well as the penis, their chiseled bodies, factories for muscles. Are you envious of my muscles? You must bow down and worship these muscles. I am everything you wish you could be.

SCENE TEN

"This is all that's left of them," says the Sister from behind, still metal-scaled and snake-like, an arm dangling out of her crotch.

She holds me by the hand and takes me away from them. Leave them with their muscles that no one can see in the dark. Out of the attic.

"It is all that the men left behind before they went away. Something for us to remember them by."

"No," I tell her. "They still continue through me. I am like a man."

"You have the parts of a man as well as a woman," says the Sister. "But you are far from masculine."

girl 28

SCENE ELEVEN

"Now what do we do?" I ask the Sister, standing there in the blank spaces.

The Sister, her blood cold under the skin, looks off-off into the empty black like it is something to look at, and she says, "You act as if there is something important we can do."

"There has to be something . . ." I tell her.

"There has never been anything important for us to do," she says to me. "We were created to fuck."

The Sister goes into the darkness to embrace the nothing that is there waiting for her, sitting down to bathe into it, to hug her knees inside of it.

"Your limbs have not fallen from you," I question the Sister. "Aren't you poisoned like the others?"

"Yes," she says. "I was one of the first to fuck Celsia."

"Then why are your arms still attached?"

The Sister rests her head into her lap, curling

eyelids down and up.

"Things will be better once we die," I tell the Sister. "Our souls will find peace, find something even better than even fucking."

And the Sister bursts into laughter, tearing laughs, crying with centipede patterns.

"Fuck toys don't have souls," she tells me, laughing and laughing, and crying.

SCENE TWELVE

I return to the hallways alone, waiting for Celsia to put
her parts back together, come back to life as a zombie
so she can fuck me again, just once more before she
goes rotten, before my own limbs fall from my body.
Or waiting for my head to fall from my neck.

The dismembered bodies are littering the floor
like dirty clothes, stepping over them and ignoring
anything that smells. The windows, I see, have disappeared entirely, eaten away from the walls, the spaces
where they stood now occupied by a patch of meat,
veiny skin stitched into the house.

In search for comfort, I climb inside of the incubator in the kitchen, the hairy cunt machine that
Celsia's ugly flesh bag was born from, curl up into a
ball and go to sleep, back to the womb now dead and
old and rotten, its warmth gone cold, crispy-black. Pretending I am inside of Celsia's cold dead cunt.

girl 29

SCENE THIRTEEN

"Look at what you've done," comes a voice from my cunt.

I curl my body inside the incubator muck, tilt-peering down to my vagina. The eyeballs have found their way inside of my cunt again, ogling back at me.

"You've brought it upon yourself," says The Something That Lives Inside of Cunts from my cunt. "The rapists were here to give you a reason to live, but now they are dead because of you."

"I don't regret the rapists," I tell my cunt. "I regret Celsia."

"You don't know what you're saying," says my cunt. "Your goal in life is to fuck as much as your body will allow before your death. You are a dildo."

"What makes me different from Celsia? Tuma? The others? Why are they so normal and I am just a soulless fuck toy?"

"You are not much different," says my cunt.

"They are also dildos. Every living being was made for fucking."

"There has to be something else to life," I tell my cunt.

"Everything else is just killing time," says my cunt. "All that matters is your sex. All that you will be remembered for is your periods of fucking."

"I want Celsia back," I tell my cunt.

"Celsia is dead," my cunt tells me, "She cannot fuck you ever again."

And I pluck the eyeballs out of my cunt and flick them out of the incubator, clicking sounds as they hit the blank kitchen floor, my eyes closing tight to remember Her, remember having sex with Her, her beautiful razor wire pubic hair.

SCENE FOURTEEN

"Get out of there," Celsia tells me, waking me from a long-long dream, her voice stained with cramps, like the mornings after drinking battery acid, a hangover. And I feel quite hungover too.

"You feel the hangover from your life," Celsia tells me. "Life was like drinking, physical pleasures made us drunk, but now we are dead and hungover."

I am dead, and I pull myself out of the incubator.

I see Celsia but something is different about her. I can't see her body, just a soul without meat, a sphere of energy, and I still want to fuck her.

"Celsia, Celsia," I groan, trying to reach out to her and rub her breast, but my hands are light and awkward and pass through Celsia's blob of body like a cloud.

She has no cunt.

I have no cock, no vagina, no tits. I am no longer

a fuck toy, but a soul. I am something above the physical. I cannot have sex.

"Why can't you fuck me?" I ask Celsia.

"We don't have the parts for it," Celsia tells me.

"I don't care," I tell Celsia. "Fuck me, fuck me, fuck me."

But she ignores. I want us to still fuck, or try to fuck. I want her soul to fuck my soul. Our vaginas still touching in spirit. But her soul just drifts away from my soul and doesn't respond to me or fuck me, fuck me, fuck me.

SCENE FIFTEEN

There's something not right about being dead. The fortress is now completely flesh, no windows or doors left, wrapped in dark warm meat and closing us deep inside, into each other. All the souls of rapists tangling up in the room, swarming each other, sad they can no longer have sex, not ever again.

This something that is not right about being dead is not only not right, but it is terribly wrong. I feel just gruesome and pathetic without skin attached, bare to the world. The sense of touch and scent and taste — everything to do with my cock and cunt — have become dead with my flesh. A soul is not that important, said The Something That Lives Inside of Cunts, and this is true. Only my cunt was important, my tits. I cannot have sex without them.

I want to be alive again.

girl 30

SCENE SIXTEEN

There are no cunts after death, so The Something That Lives Inside of Cunts is not here, and cannot answer my questions.

Our souls are just stored in this little container which has no resemblance to the fortress anymore, squeezed together in a crowd, glowing spheres of some energy similar to light but cannot be seen by the living. I cannot tell which soul is Celsia's anymore, there are so many and we all are the same, no one speaks, just dizzy-swirling around each other still looking for a way to fuck.

No sign of Heaven, nor any God.

Just a tight space.

girl 34

SCENE SEVENTEEN

Eventually, something happens.

A quaking outside of the container, rumbling and all the walls are vibrating, the rapists swarming faster now, leaving tracers behind them.

And then flying serpents, out of the walls these large white snakes ripple through the room to us. They begin to swallow us. One snake to one soul/meal. The snakes expand their jaws and gulp down spheres, leaving large bulges in their heads.

We try to get away from them, but they are quick and we are trapped inside of this little room, the walls still quaking all around us, faster-faster, makes us disoriented but this is very natural to the hungry snakes.

From behind, without a chance to react, a mouth wraps around me. I can see it from all angles as it squeezes me inside of it, closes its lips over me.

Something has swallowed me whole and it wasn't even Celsia's cunt, closing my eyes (or whatever's on my soul that acts as eyes) pretending I really have been eaten by Celsia's cunt, the snake's teeth like Celsia's razor wire pubic hair.

SCENE EIGHTEEN

When my eyes open, I can see stuff-headed snakes all around me, their white bodies scurrying in circles, the walls still quaking violence around us.

The snake's eyes have become my eyes, my body has become the snake's body. Things are physical once again. I feel like matter instead of energy. And the others notice this, hoping their new bodies have parts to fuck with, swirling around each other looking for holes.

And the rumbling gets so violent until it explodes, all around us a whoosh of explosion, and we are blown out of our little room, through the hallway of the factory, the long meaty shaft, blown out of there by the force of the explosion. And then a new sexual urge creeps up inside me as I go hurling through the meaty walls.

Something seductive in the far distance. Not a cunt, but something just as exciting, using my new snake body to swim through the air towards it. The others feel this sensation as well, all of us heading in the same direction to get to it first. Swimming/flying as fast as we can, only one of us can have it, only one can fuck it.

SCENE NINETEEN

Inside of a new place, new warm place. The others dead somewhere outside, their soul energy slurped up inside of my new home, the meat walls absorbing their lifeforce. But I am not alone in here, somebody else survived.

Celsia is with me.

I cannot see her, but I know she is here with me, next to me. For some reason, we both made it inside, to be together.

She doesn't speak, but she will eventually. We will have a new life together, new bodies with each other.

I cannot wait for us to be born again, so that we can fuck again and again and again.

I have dreams of cunts getting wet, cocks getting hard.

Someone far away is watching me from outside of my dreams, licking His lips at me and masturbating all over Himself.

(note: Carlton Mellick III does not have two heads in real life, we just gave him two heads in this picture because it looks pretty cool. Don't you agree?)

ABOUT THE AUTHOR

Carlton Mellick III is a bizarrist author of several books you probably haven't heard of before, such as *Satan Burger*, *Electric Jesus Corpse*, *Sunset with a Beard*, and *The Baby Jesus Butt Plug*. He lives in Portland, OR, where he drinks hot sauce and manages an eyebrow farm. Visit him at his website which might be www.avantpunk.com or maybe www.sexycarl.com or something stupid like that.

ABOUT THE COVER ARTIST

Steven Stahlberg is an award-winning computer artist who created Webbie Tookay, the first virtual woman sponsored by a major modeling agency. Take a tour of his online art galleries at www.optidigit.com/stevens

ERASERHEAD PRESS BOOKS
www.eraserheadpress.com

Eraserhead Press is a collective publishing organization with a mission to create a new genre for "bizarre" literature. A genre that brings together the neo-surrealists, the post-postmodernists, the literary punks, the magical realists, the masters of grotesque fantasy, the bastards of offbeat horror, and all other rebels of the written word. Together, these authors fight to tear down convention, explode from the underground, and create a new era in alternative literature. All the elements that make independent films "cult" films are displayed twice as wildly in this fiction series. Eraserhead Press strives to be your major source for bizarre/cult fiction.

SOME THINGS ARE BETTER LEFT UNPLUGGED
by Vincent W. Sakowski.
A post-modern fantasy filled with anti-heroes and anti-climaxes. An allegorical tale, the story satirizes many of our everyday obsessions, including: the pursuit of wealth and materialism;the thirst for empty spectacles and violence; and climbing whatever social, political, or economical ladder is before us. Join the man and his Nemesis, the obese tabby, and a host of others for a nightmare roller coaster ride from realm to realm, microcosm to microcosm: The Carnival, The Fray, The Garden of Earthly Delights, and The Court of The Crimson Ey'd King. Pretentious gobbledygook or an unparalleled anti-epic of the surreal and absurd? Read on and find out.

ISBN: 0-9713572-2-6, 156 pages, trade paperback: $9.95

SZMONHFU
by Hertzan Chimera
Fear the machine - it is changing. The change comes not only from the manner of my life but from the manner of my death. I will die four deaths; the death of the flesh; the death of the soul; the death of myth; the death of reason and all of those deaths will contain the seed of resurrection. This is the time of the stomach. This is the time when we expand as a single cell expands. The flesh grows but the psyche does not grow. That is life.

ISBN: 0-9713572-4-2, 284 pages, trade paperback $15.95

THE KAFKA EFFEKT
by D. Harlan Wilson

A collection of forty-four short stories loosely written in the vein of Franz Kafka, with more than a pinch of William S. Burroughs sprinkled on top. A manic depressive has a baby's bottom grafted onto his face; a hermaphrodite impregnates itself and gives birth to twins; a gaggle of professors find themselves trapped in a port-a-john and struggle to liberate their minds from the prison of reason—these are just a few of the precarious situations that the characters herein are forced to confront. The Kafka Effekt is a postmodern scream. Absurd, intelligent, funny and scatological, Wilson turns reality inside out and exposes it as a grotesque, nightmarish machine that is always-already processing the human subject, who struggles to break free from the machine, but who at the same time revels in its subjugation.
ISBN: 0-9713572-1-8, 216 pages, trade paperback: $13.95

SATAN BURGER
by Carlton Mellick III

A collage of absurd philosophies and dark surrealism, written and directed by Carlton Mellick III, starring a colorful cast of squatter punks on a journey to find their place in a world that doesn't want them anymore. Featuring: a city overrun with peoples from other dimensions, a narrator who sees his body from a third-person perspective, a man whose flesh is dead but his body parts are alive and running amok, an overweight messiah, the personal life of the Grim Reaper, lots of classy sex and violence, and a fast food restaurant owned by the devil himself. 2001, Approx. 236 min., Color, Hi-Fi Stereo, Rated R.
ISBN: 0-9713572-3-4, 236 pages, trade paperback: $14.95

SHALL WE GATHER AT THE GARDEN?
by Kevin L. Donihe

"It illuminates. It demonizes. It pulls the strings of the puppets controlling the strangest of passion plays within a corporate structure. Everyone, every thing is a target of Mr. Donihe's wit and off-kilter worldview . . . There are shades of Philip K. Dick's wonderfully inventive The Divine Invasion (minus the lurid pop singer), trading up Zen Buddhism for unconscious Gnosticism. Malachi manifests where Elijah would stand revealed; and the Roald Dahl-like midgets hold the pink laser beam shining into our hero's mind. Religion is lambasted under the scrutiny of Corporate money-crunchers, and nothing is what it seems." - From the introduction by Jeffrey A. Stadt
ISBN: 0-9713572-5-0, 244 pages, trade paperback: $14.95

MY DREAM DATE (RAPE) WITH KATHY ACKER
by Michael Hemmingson
In this new collection of fictions—a handful of small tales and two novellas—Michael Hemmingson retains his notorious status as the subversive prince of the avant-pop; or, as stated in The American Book Review, "one of the reckless youths of a quick and dirty literature."
Sex, drugs, Raymond Carver's ghost, Barbie dolls loving GI Joe dolls, the pure vaginas of French girls, the un-pure vagina of Kathy Acker, crack whores, nutty neighbors, scatological girlfriends, iniquitous fiends, Jesus freaks, pornographers, pushers, movers, shakers and winning lottery tickets are just some of the topics found in this unique book that is certain to titillate and aggravate the finest minds of the 21st Century.
ISBN: 0-9713572-9-3, 176 pages, trade paperback: $10.95 us

SKIN PRAYER
fragments of abject memory by Doug Rice
Doug Rice is haunted-by what we can only guess. He is trapped; he goes nowhere. He is a modern day hysteric, a psychoanalyst's dream. He writes the same thing over and over, runs the same spinning track, as if somehow, through the repetition of extremes, he could eliminate the trauma, break its foul-smelling, icy-fingered spell. Only it is a spell of beauty —the beauty that comes from devastation, from the constant struggle to rise again in that roaring fire's shouldered wake. You will find no plot or answers here, only the unbearable loss of abandonment and grief. Make no mistake: Doug Rice kills us again and again and he does not want us to survive it, for he has been burned at the stake and is burning still. He is a ghost who can do nothing but plead with his bones and remind us with the choking beauty ghosts bring. Despite his pleas, you will not like him. You will not like him, and yet . . .Skin Prayer is the power of redemption in the word when life has failed us. It has no inside or outside, it is only itself. It is the self-enclosed, hermetic world of obsessive need, a space where one can't breath. And yet it is breath. In its own suffocated space, if we survive it, or are patient enough not to throw it aside, it gives us insufferable hope.
Leslie Heywood, Associate Professor of English & Cultural Studies
ISBN: 0-9713572-7-7, 237 pages, trade paperback: $14.95

COMING SOON
Lance Olsen, D. Harlan Wilson, Hertzan Chimera,
M. F. Korn, Harold Jaffe, Richard Harland, and Jeffrey Stadt

LaVergne, TN USA
16 April 2010
179543LV00001B/94/A